A Picture Book for Grown-Up Children

Written by C. B. Bryza

Illustrated by Simon Greiner

Gallery Books
New York London Toronto Sydney New Delhi

G

Gallery Books
A Division of Simon & Schuster, Inc.
1230 Avenue of the Americas
New York, NY 10020

This book is a work of fiction. Any references to historical events, real people, or real places are used fictitiously. Other names, characters, places, and events are products of the author's imagination, and any resemblance to actual events or places or persons, living or dead, is entirely coincidental.

First Gallery Books hardcover edition February 2014

Designed by Joy O'Meara

Manufactured in the United States of America

1 3 5 7 9 10 8 6 4 2

Library of Congress Cataloging-in-Publication Data is available.

ISBN 978-1-4767-3155-1
ISBN 978-1-4767-3156-8 (ebook)

To My Soul Mate

A young woman bit her lip.

YOU'RE
INVITED

COOK
SAVE THE DATE
Wedding
We're getting

She had a strong sense
of self-worth.
BILL
She had financial
independence.

She had fantastic friends and family.

She had a life purpose
and a heart
full of love.

She did not have
a boyfriend.

"Where is my boyfriend?"
she said.

She wanted to
share her life with
someone special.

But where was that someone?

"I will go and look for him," she said.

So away she went.

31

She went with a friend to a party,
and there she saw a tough guy.

"Are you my boyfriend?"
she said to the tough guy.

The tough guy just looked and looked.
He did not say a thing.

The tough guy was not her boyfriend,
so she went on.

Then she met a
wealthy cad.

He said she was sexy and made lots of promises.

“Are you my boyfriend?”
she asked the wealthy cad.

“I am not your boyfriend.
I’m emotionally unavailable,”
said the wealthy cad.

The tough guy was not her boyfriend.

The wealthy cad was not her boyfriend.

So the young woman went on.

Next she came to an artsy lad.
He had soft hands and kind eyes.

“Are you my boyfriend?”
she asked the
artsy lad.

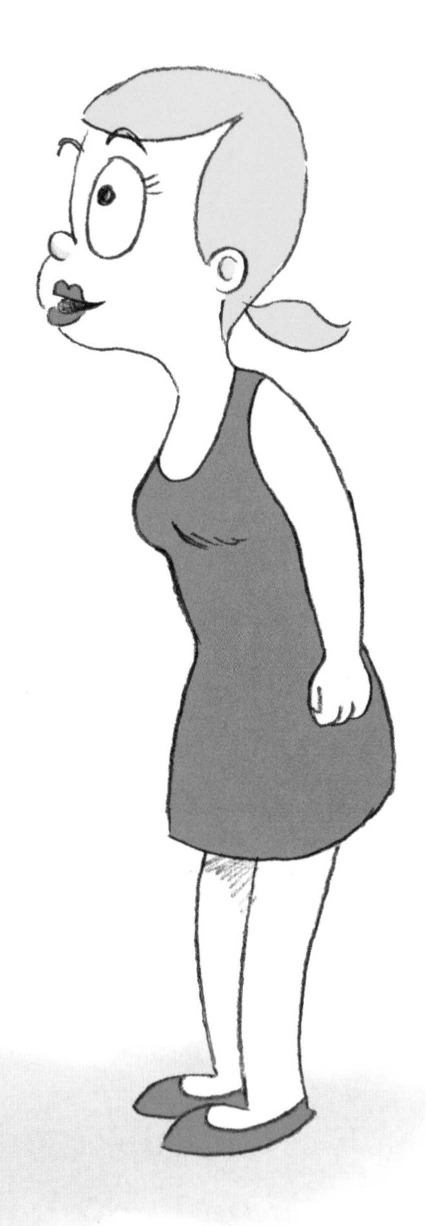

The artsy lad gave her a winsome smile.
“I’m not your boyfriend,” he told her.
“I’m more into my craft.”

She turned to an average dude.

"Are you my boyfriend?" she asked him.

The average dude seemed nice enough.

But no.
"I'm not your boyfriend," he said.

"I'm more into your friend."

The tough guy
and the wealthy cad
were not her boyfriend.

The artsy lad and
the average dude
were not her boyfriend.

So the young woman went on.

She saw two striking men in a corner.

Maybe one of them was her boyfriend!

“Are you—or you—my boyfriend?”
she asked the men.

"I'm married—"

"—and I'm gay," said the men.

Neither man was her boyfriend.

The young woman worried.

Would she ever have a boyfriend?

“I will have a boyfriend,”
she said.
“I know I will. I will!
I just have to keep looking.”

Soon the young
woman agreed to
a blind date.

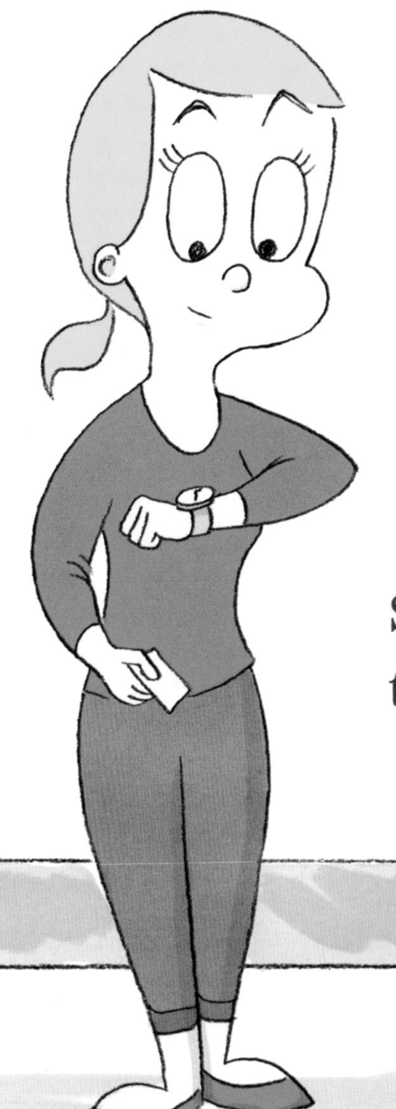

She waited in front of
the theater.

She waited and waited for her date.
But he did not come, the flake.

The flake was not her boyfriend.

At least the movie
was good.

"Perhaps my boyfriend is in the park," said the young woman.

So she went for a walk.

She was glad, because she smelled flowers and tasted fresh air and felt sunshine and heard laughter.

But she did not see her boyfriend.

At a coffee shop,
the young woman
spotted a fellow whose
shirt was wrinkled.

"Excuse me," she said.

"Are you by chance my boyfriend?"

He gave a long sigh.
"I'm afraid not,"
he said.

“I’m still
in love
with my ex.”

“I’m sorry,”
the young woman said,
and she went on.

She went into a bookstore.

She spent a long time
in the self-help section,
but she did not feel better.

SPECIAL

The young woman was tired of looking for her boyfriend.

She wanted to go home and relax.

Maybe with some cookies.

The young woman settled into her favorite chair.

Just then she heard a knock on the door.

"Who is it?" she asked.

Looking through the peephole,
she could see it was her neighbor.

She opened the door.

"I thought I smelled cookies baking," said her neighbor. He held up a jug of milk.

"Would you like some company?"

She stared at her neighbor.
He smiled.

"Do you know who I am?" he asked.

"Yes, I know who you are,"
the young woman said.

“You are not a tough guy.

“You are not a wealthy cad.

“You are not an artsy lad
and you are not an average dude.

“You are not gay or married
or a flake or in love with your ex.

“And you are not my boyfriend.

"You are my soul mate!"